JUMPING MOUSE

A Native American Legend of Friendship and Sacrifice

JUMPING
MOUSE

A Native American Legend of Friendship and Sacrifice

MISTY SCHROE

PAGE
STREET
KIDS

INTRODUCTION

One of my favorite roles when I was little was as the storyteller's daughter. I remember traveling with my mom to schools and camps and helping her set up before she began to tell her stories. I would fold her blanket, unravel her story string, or arrange seating in a circle around her. A simple classroom would suddenly change to a sacred place with my mom's first step into the room, blanket over her arm, walking to the beat of the drum. I would wear one of her old Native dresses and sit cross-legged on a blanket in the corner, watching silently as she walked to the center of the room, placed her blanket in front of her, and said, "I am Laughing Bird and I welcome you to my blanket." Old Native American tales would be brought to life in the oral tradition, each one with memorable characters and a subtle lesson on life or community.

My favorite of her tales was "Jumping Mouse," the story of a tiny mouse that dreamed of a better place. It always gave me great hope, as I was a very small child and the youngest of my family. I felt tiny and insignificant, but Jumping Mouse was small and she could give what little she had to help those around her, and in return they would help her. In the end, through many trials, she achieved her dream, and it was more than she could have even imagined. This gave me hope that even though right now might be hard, the future is bright with endless possibilities. Knowing that you can make a difference in people's lives, no matter how little you are, was a lesson I very much took to heart.

We all have a voice to be heard; we just speak in different ways.

Long, long ago, there was a mouse.

She was a mouse like any other mouse—nose to the ground, running here and there, only seeing what was right in front of her. Except for one difference: she had a dream.

She had heard a story the old ones told about somewhere far away, the High Places where life was good, and she dreamed of going there. "Come with me!" she said to the other mice. "There is a better place for us!" But they did not want a different life.

So, all alone, she went to find the High Places.

She scurried along until she came to a river. The water was running fast and looked deep. How would she get across? Then she heard a low, raspy voice: "Hello."

Jumping in shock, the mouse looked around and saw a large frog sitting under a leaf. "Hello," she responded, tilting her head in curiosity.

"Who are you and where are you going?" asked the mysterious frog.

"Oh, I am just a mouse like any other mouse . . . but I have a dream. I am going to the High Places! They are beyond anything I can imagine, but I know I can get there."

"I am Grandfather Frog," rumbled the frog. "I know of the High Places and am touched by the eagerness of your heart. Your journey will be long and hard, but because of your great longing I will give you a gift to help you. Close your eyes."

The mouse squeezed her eyes shut and heard Grandfather Frog say, "Jump! Jump as high as you can!" The little mouse crouched down and jumped. As she did, she felt her legs grow longer . . . and longer!

"Your new name is Jumping Mouse. For with these long legs you will cover much distance," cried Grandfather Frog.

Jumping Mouse opened her eyes to see her wonderful new long legs. She turned to thank the frog, but he had disappeared.

"I wish I could have told him how grateful I am, for now I can surely cross the river," she said to herself, and jumped over the water.

The wide, grassy plains started on the other side of the river.

"Now my journey has truly begun!" thought Jumping Mouse. She hopped and hopped and hopped, until she was very hot and tired. Looking for a cool place to rest, she noticed a massive mound in the middle of the grass. As she inched closer to shelter under its shade . . . it moved!

It was a buffalo! Jumping Mouse sat very still because she was afraid that she would be stepped on. Timidly, she looked up and was surprised to see that the buffalo was crying.

"Brother Buffalo, why are you crying?" she asked.

"I have lost my sight," said the huge buffalo. "And without my eyes, I cannot tell which grasses are good and which will poison me, so I will die."

Great pity filled Jumping Mouse's heart as she rested her paw on Brother Buffalo. "I am so sorry for your loss, but do not fear! My name is Jumping Mouse and your journey has not ended yet, for I will give you a gift. You will now be known as Eyes-of-a-Mouse!"

Suddenly, the buffalo could see, but, to Jumping Mouse's surprise, the world had gone dark all around her, as if twilight had fallen on a moonless night. For in giving the buffalo this new name, she had given him her own sight.

Jumping Mouse could hear Eyes-of-a-Mouse rumbling with joyous laughter as he rushed through the grass in circles, and she smiled wholeheartedly.

The buffalo exclaimed, "I would like to thank you! Is there anything I can do for you?"

"I must cross the plains to go to the mountains where the High Places are, but I cannot see," said Jumping Mouse. "Will you be my guide?"

So together they traveled across the plains until they reached the foot of the mountain. "I am sorry, but this is as far as I can go. For this is the end of the plains and I was not made to travel up the mountain," said Eyes-of-a-Mouse.

"I understand," said Jumping Mouse. "I cannot see, but I can smell the crisp air of the mountain. I have hope I will find the High Places!" So, saying goodbye to the buffalo, she went on.

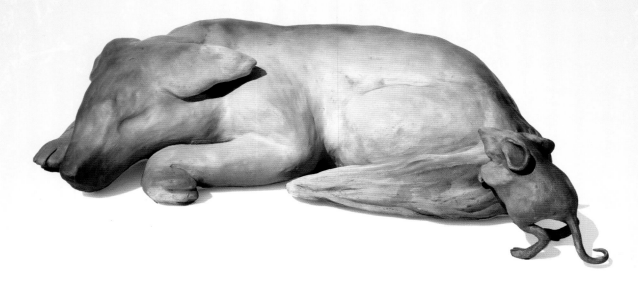

Jumping Mouse knew the mountain rose high before her.

The sweet smell of grass was now replaced by the strong scent of pine and moss. Holding her dream close to her heart, she took a breath and started to climb. Feeling her way around tree roots and following the scent of the mountain breeze, she hopped and hopped and hopped until she was very hot and tired. Panting for breath, she felt a soft object with a large shadow, where it was cool. As she leaned up against it . . . it moved!

It was a wolf! Jumping Mouse sat very still because she was afraid that she would be eaten. In the silence, she could hear the wolf crying. Crawling closer to the sound, Jumping Mouse bravely asked, "Sister Wolf, why are you crying?"

"I have lost my sense of smell," said the wolf. "Without my nose, I cannot hunt, so I will die."

Jumping Mouse's fear was replaced with pity, and, reaching out, she placed a comforting paw on Sister Wolf's face. "I am so sorry for your loss, but do not fear! My name is Jumping Mouse, and your journey has not ended yet, for I can give you a gift. You will now be known as Nose-of-a-Mouse!"

Suddenly, the wolf could smell all the things of the earth around her, but as Jumping Mouse suspected, she herself could no longer smell the crisp mountain air. She could not sense anything beyond her reach. For she had given the wolf not only a new name, but also her own sense of smell. Jumping Mouse could hear Nose-of-a-Mouse's joyous howl at the return of her precious sense and she lovingly smiled. The path ahead may be more challenging now, but the joy she was able to give was worth it.

Nose-of-a-Mouse said, "I would like to thank you for such a wondrous gift! Is there anything I can do for you?"

"I must climb the mountain to find the High Places, and I cannot see or smell the way," Jumping Mouse said. "Will you be my guide?" So, together, they climbed higher and higher up the mountain.

As they reached the tree line, Jumping Mouse could feel the crisp wind getting stronger. She could hear the soft scraping of Nose-of-a-Mouse's claws as the dirt gave way to solid rock and knew they were near the top.

"I am sorry, but this is as far as I can go. For this is the end of my territory, and there is no cover or food for me above the tree line," said Nose-of-a-Mouse.

"I understand," said Jumping Mouse. "I cannot see and I cannot smell, but I have a dream. I will find the High Places!" So, saying goodbye to the wolf, she went on.

But the journey was now very hard. Poor Jumping Mouse could not see and she could not smell, so she did not know where she was and did not know where to go. All the mountain rocks felt the same under her small paws, and all she could hear was the howling of the wind. Slowly, she stopped hopping and sat very still. A little tear found its way down her cheek. She was so very lost. How would she find the High Places now?

Suddenly she heard a raspy croak: "Jumping Mouse, why are you crying?"

She knew that voice! It was Grandfather Frog! "I have a dream to go to the High Places," cried Jumping Mouse, "but since I cannot see and cannot smell, I do not know where to go!"

"Fear not, Jumping Mouse, for I will give you one more gift," said Grandfather Frog. "Jump! Jump now, as high as you can!"

So, Jumping Mouse crouched down and she jumped! Higher and higher she went, and, behind her, she heard Grandfather Frog rumble, "Jumping Mouse, because you have selflessly given all that was special to you, I give you the gift of Freedom and Great Sight. You will live in the High Places. Open your eyes!"

Jumping Mouse opened her eyes and saw an endless blue sky, bright with sunlight. Her body felt weightless as she glided on the wind. Below, she saw the world spread out before her; there was no limit to where she could go. With great exhilaration she soared higher and heard Grandfather Frog's voice echoing all around her, "For I have named you . . .

EAGLE!"

THE ARTISTIC PROCESS

Ceramics are very complex. For me, it's all about finding a balance between control and trust. Like the artist Michelangelo, I believe in the concept of releasing the sculpture from its organic form rather than the idea that the sculpture is simply an object of my creation. I like to think of each of my pieces as living, in a way. So, once I have a basic idea of form and balance, I start to build. Meditating on the character's personality, I coil build the body. Sometimes I'll just get a sense that there is negative space that needs to be filled or some part that needs to be taken away. It's all about listening to subtleties of the clay and using my skills to accomplish them. With a lot of patience and controlled drying, my ceramic babies are born. I prefer to use a more natural surface treatment, mostly iron oxide or smoke fired.

Then it's all about finding the right location and taking thousands of photos from several angles, sometimes on multiple days, and editing them. I drive up mountains, hike through trails, and even wade through streams, carrying my ceramics to achieve the perfect shot. It's such a great adventure every time.

To my grandfather.

First published in 2019 by Page Street Kids,
an imprint of
Page Street Publishing Co.
27 Congress Street, Suite 105
Salem, MA 01970
www.pagestreetpublishing.com

Distributed by Macmillan, sales in Canada by The Canadian Manda Group

19 20 21 22 23 CCO 5 4 3 2 1

ISBN-13: 978-1-62414-817-0 ISBN-10: 1-62414-817-4
CIP data for this book is available from the Library of Congress.

This book was typeset in Plantgenet Cheroke.
The figures were made with clay and photographed on location in New Hampshire.
Printed and bound in Shenzhen, Guangdong, China

Page Street Publishing uses only materials from suppliers who are committed to
responsible and sustainable forest management.

Page Street Publishing protects our planet by donating to nonprofits like The Trustees,
which focuses on local land conservation.

t
trustees